TOO MANY TURNERS

by Wendy Wax
illustrated by Harry Moore

Ready-to-Read

Simon Spotlight/Nickelodeon
New York   London   Toronto   Sydney

Based on the TV series *The Fairly OddParents*®
created by Butch Hartman as seen on Nickelodeon®

SIMON SPOTLIGHT
An imprint of Simon & Schuster Children's Publishing Division
1230 Avenue of the Americas, New York, New York 10020

Copyright © 2004 Viacom International Inc. All rights reserved.
NICKELODEON, *The Fairly OddParents*, and all related titles, logos,
and characters are registered trademarks of Viacom International Inc.
All rights reserved, including the right of reproduction in whole
or in part in any form. Nelvana is the International Representative.
NELVANA® Nelvana Limited. CORUS™ Corus Entertainment Inc.
All rights reserved.
Manufactured in the United States of America

READY-TO-READ, SIMON SPOTLIGHT, and colophon
are registered trademarks of Simon & Schuster.

First Edition
2 4 6 8 10 9 7 5 3 1

Library of Congress Cataloging-in-Publication Data

Wax, Wendy.
Too many Turners / by Wendy Wax.—1st ed.
p. cm.—(Ready-to-read)
"Based on the TV show The Fairly OddParents created by
Butch Hartman as seen on Nickelodeon."
Summary: When Cosmo and Wanda grant Timmy's wish for lots of
brothers and sisters to play with, things get a bit crowded.
ISBN 0-689-86859-6 (pbk.)
[1. Brothers and sisters—Fiction. 2. Wishes—Fiction.
3. Fairies—Fiction.]
I. Fairly OddParents (Television program) II. Title. III. Series.
PZ7.W35117 To 2004
[E]–dc22
2003022784

It was Saturday. Timmy Turner
had the whole day ahead of him.
After breakfast he set out for
Chester's house.

Chester was making lemonade.

"Hey, Chester," Timmy said.

"Want to go to the park?"

"I can't," said Chester.

"We are having a family reunion.

One hundred relatives
are coming over.
Thirty-four are already here."
"Wow!" said Timmy.

Timmy went to A.J.'s house.

A.J. was on his bike.

"Want to go to the park?"

Timmy asked.

"I can't," said A.J. "We are going on a family bike ride and then watching family movies."

"Too bad," said Timmy.

Timmy went home. "Can we have a
family day?" he asked his parents.
"Not today," said Mr. Turner.
"We are going to our 'Spending
Saturdays with Your Child' class."

"So we will know how to spend time
with you!" said Mrs. Turner.
"Vicky is coming to babysit."
Timmy groaned.

Timmy tried playing alone,
but it was no fun.
He tried working on his
monster robot, but the eyes
would not light up.

"You look bored," said Cosmo.

"Are you okay?" Wanda asked.

"Being an only child sure is lonely,"
Timmy said to his fairy godparents.

"How can you be lonely with us around all the time?" asked Cosmo.

"Yeah, sweetie. You always have us!" added Wanda.

"I know, but I can't play with you anywhere I want to. I have to keep you a secret," said Timmy.

Poof!

"I wish I had lots of brothers and
sisters to play with," Timmy said.
POOF! Cosmo and Wanda made
his wish come true.

"Hey, big brother," called a boy.

"Big brother?" said Timmy,
liking the sound of it. He looked
around. Kids of all ages
were everywhere, and they
looked a lot like him.

"Welcome to my family, person
who looks like me!" said Timmy.

One of Timmy's older sisters
inspected his monster robot.
"It will not light up," he told her.
"These wires need to touch,"
said the girl. "Like this."
The robot's eyes lit up.
"Thanks, big sis!" said Timmy.

"Will you read to us?" asked
Timmy's little brothers and sisters.
"Sure," said Timmy. He found his
favorite issue of The Crimson Chin
and began to read when . . . CRASH!

The sound came from Timmy's
bedroom. "Oh, no!" he cried.

His robot was broken.

"It was an accident," said a boy
with a tennis racquet.

Timmy saw a baby chewing on his favorite Crimson Chin action figure. "Stop that!" he yelled, but it was no use.

The house was noisy, crowded, and messy.

"I wish I were an only child again," Timmy said.

But nothing happened. Timmy looked around for Cosmo and Wanda—but the fishbowl was gone!

Timmy's parents came in.

They looked tired and frazzled.

"Can we borrow some money?"

Mrs. Turner asked Timmy.

"You want to borrow money

from me?" Timmy asked.

"We will need help paying Vicky," explained Mr. Turner. "Her rates went up because of all of your brothers and sisters." Sadly, Timmy handed over his piggy bank.

Timmy went downstairs.

"Hi, Tommy!" Vicky said sweetly.

"It's Timmy," said Timmy. Then he realized Vicky had been talking to

his older brother Tommy.

Vicky didn't even try to boss Timmy
around. She didn't read stories
or offer snacks, either.
All she did was try to get
Tommy's attention.
In a weird way, Timmy missed
Vicky's attention.

25

"Cosmo! Wanda!" Timmy shouted,

pushing through a crowd of siblings.

"What?" asked a boy named Cosmo.

"Yes?" asked a girl named Wanda.

26 "Never mind," Timmy said, sighing.

Upstairs, Timmy found a girl
trying on his mom's makeup.
"Have you seen my fishbowl?"
he asked her. Just then he
heard something in the bathroom.

A set of triplets dangled the fairy
godparents above the toilet.
"Fish are icky!" they said. Cosmo
and Wanda squirmed to get loose.

Timmy grabbed Cosmo and Wanda.
"I wish I were an only child again,"
he said quickly.
Cosmo and Wanda were happy to
grant his wish. POOF!

"Are you lonely without brothers
and sisters to play with?"
Wanda asked.
"Not at all," said Timmy.
"I will never be lonely
with you two around!"
Cosmo and Wanda smiled proudly.

Just then Vicky stormed in.
"It looks like a hurricane hit
this house," she shouted.
"Clean it—NOW!"
"Okay," said Timmy. He didn't
have anything better to do
on this Saturday afternoon.

While Timmy was cleaning,

Chester called.

"My cousins want to meet you,"

he said. "Can you come over?"

"Oh, brother!" said Timmy.

"I'm not in a family sort of mood."

Cosmo screamed. "Please, Timmy!

Don't say the word 'brother'

for a long time!"